Kathy's Hats
A story of hope

Trudy Krisher

Illustrated by
Nadine Bernard Westcott

ALBERT WHITMAN & COMPANY • Morton Grove, Illinois

With love to
the children and teachers
at Edwin D. Smith School
and with hope to
Tiffany, David, Karri, Shelley, Jason, Spencer, Heather, Jana,
and, of course, Kathy.
T.K.

To all children
who have struggled against cancer.
N.B.W.

The illustrations are watercolor and ink.
The text typeface is Palatino.
Design by Lucy Smith.

Text © 1992 by Trudy Krisher.
Illustrations © 1992 by Nadine Bernard Westcott.
Published in 1992 by Albert Whitman & Company,
6340 Oakton Street, Morton Grove, Illinois 60053.
All rights reserved. No part of this book may be reproduced or transmitted
in any form or by any means, electronic or mechanical, including
photocopying, recording, or by any information storage and retrieval
system, without permission in writing from the publisher.
Printed in China
10   9   8   7

Library of Congress Cataloging-in-Publication Data
Krisher, Trudy.
Kathy's hats: a story of hope/Trudy Krisher;
Illustrated by Nadine Bernard Westcott.
p.   cm.
Summary: Kathy's love of hats comes in handy
when the chemotherapy treatments she receives
for her cancer make her hair fall out.
ISBN 0-8075-4116-8
[1. Cancer—Fiction. 2. Hats—Fiction.]
I. Westcott, Nadine Bernard, Ill. II. Title.
PZ7.K8967Kat 1992   92-2659
[Fic]—dc20   CIP
                                         AC

When I was born,
I was almost bald.
My mother tied
a tiny green ribbon
to my little puff of fuzz.
This was my first hat.

My second hat was a woolen
cap my grandmother knitted.
It had flaps that covered my ears,
and it came with a pair
of matching booties.

At the beach, my bonnet
kept the sun out of my eyes
when I played in the sand.

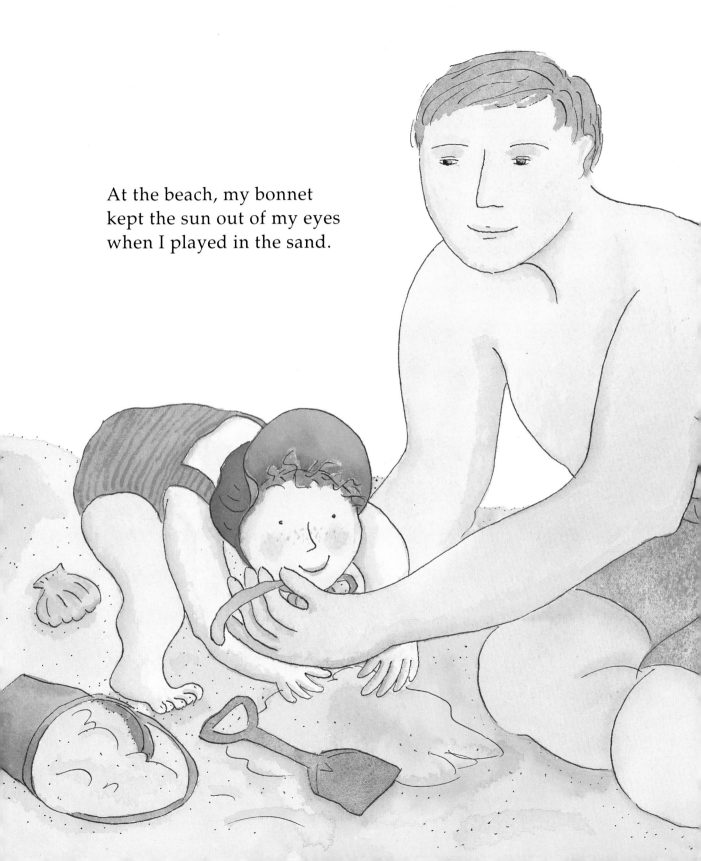

When I was four,
I liked wearing
the velvet hat
in my dress-up box.
It had a veil
that came down
over my eyes.

Hats were fun, and they stood
for special times in my life.
One Easter, I wore a white straw boater
with a blue ribbon around the brim.
That was the year I found seventeen eggs
and a chocolate bunny at the Easter egg hunt.

When I started to play tennis,
I wore a hat with an eyeshade
that kept the glare off my face.

The day I finally learned to swim,
I wore a purple bathing cap.

At my first ball game,
my father bought me a program,
a hot dog with extra mustard,
and a baseball hat.

Then, one year, something happened to me.
It was something that doesn't happen
to many children, but it happened to me.
That something was a very serious disease.
Its name was cancer.

Because of the cancer,
sometimes I felt sick,

sometimes I felt mad,

and sometimes
I felt scared that I might die.

I had to miss lots of school.
I had to go to the hospital
to take strong medicine
in a treatment called chemotherapy.

I didn't like it
when they poked me
with a needle
to put the medicine in.
I yelled, "Ouch!"
and squeezed
my mom's hand real tight.

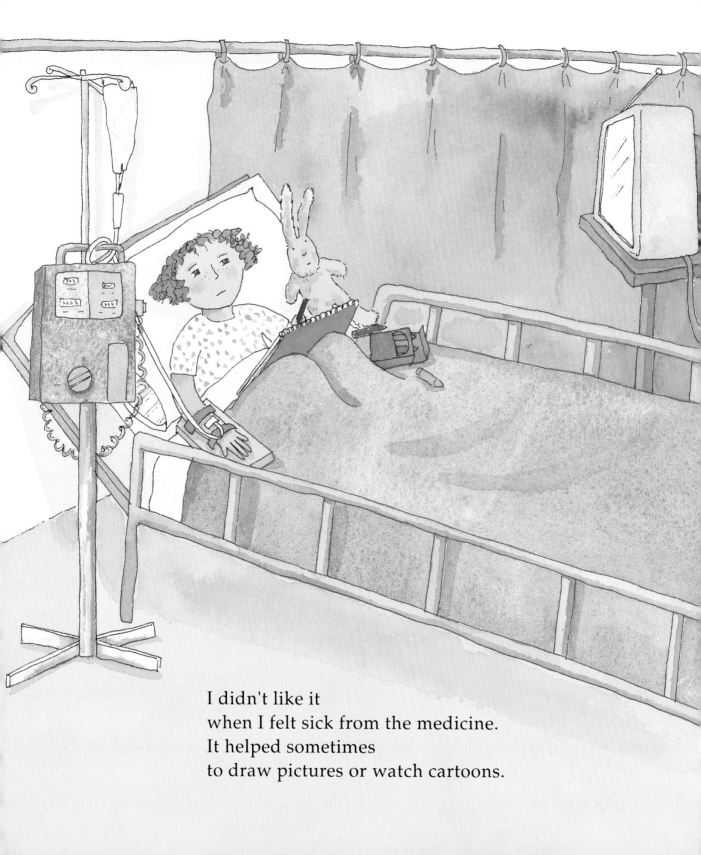

I didn't like it
when I felt sick from the medicine.
It helped sometimes
to draw pictures or watch cartoons.

But the worst thing about the medicine
was that it made my hair fall out.
Little by little, I began shedding,
just like my cat, Mittens.
Soon I was bald again,
as bald as when I was a baby.
I hated it!

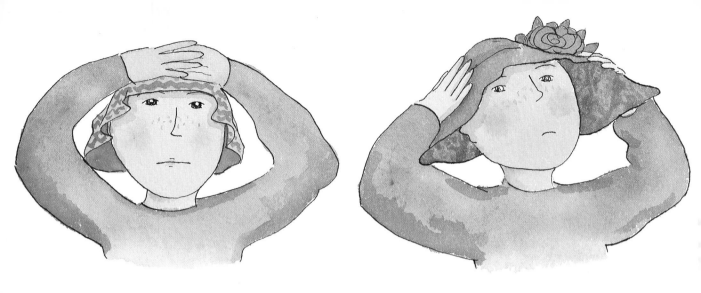

My mother bought me lots of hats
to cover my bald head.
I wore them, but I didn't like them.
I was embarrassed!
I felt different from my friends.
They had bangs and barrettes
and ponytails and curls.
All *I* had was hats.

When I got cancer, many things changed for me,
even how I felt about hats.

Here is my class picture from that year.
Annie is in the green sweater.
She is my best friend.

Edward is the tall one in the back.
He got glasses last summer.
Adrianne is the tiny one in front
on the very end.
When Mrs. Hofmann asked us
to write a story about wishes,
Adrianne wished that she would grow.
I wished that I had my hair back.
Do you see me there in the middle?
I'm smiling in the picture,
but I'm not smiling inside.

I'm the one in the dumb hat.

I complained about my hats a lot.
One morning my mother said that maybe
I wasn't wearing the most important hat of all.
The most important hat, she said,
is something called a thinking cap.

A thinking cap is invisible.
But it is something you put on
to help you think when you are
faced with a challenge. My mother said
that the most important thing about a person
is the way she thinks about things.

I thought about what my mother had said
while I pinned my teddy bear pin to my shirt.
This was something I did every day.
My friend Meaghan had given me the bear
on my last birthday. My name is written
across the bear's fat brown tummy.

I thought about
how happy
the bear looked
and what I had just learned
about the thinking cap.
So I tried something
different that morning.
I pinned my teddy bear pin
to my hat.
I thought it might
make my hat
look happier.
It did!

Everyone liked the bear on my hat.
At Halloween, my friend Kim gave me a pin
of a ghost and a jack-o'-lantern.
I put it on my hat.
At Christmas, my teacher gave me
a Santa Claus pin.

When I had to go to a special hospital in Minnesota,
my parents got me a pin shaped like the state.
In February, the nurses at the hospital where I had
radiation therapy pinned a Valentine's heart to my hat.

Soon I had a lot of pins, and I began to like this hat.
I wore it every day, to school and for my treatments.
Sometimes I even forgot that I was bald.

We had a celebration in school last week!
My teacher asked my mother to bring in cupcakes,
and she told everyone to wear a hat.
Almost two years had passed since I got sick,
and I had some important news to tell.

I grinned when I said
my chemotherapy treatments were over
and the doctors thought my cancer had gone away.

Everybody cheered,
and then the whole class
threw their hats in the air—

including me!

I'll always have a thinking cap,
but I'm excited about going on to other hats . . .

when I graduate,

when I get married,

or, someday, when I pick out hats
for a child of my own.

Author's Note

My daughter Kathy was nine years old when she began to complain about pain in her arm. Her doctor recommended an X-ray, and a biopsy confirmed my worst fears. Kathy had cancer—Ewing's sarcoma, a rare bone cancer that typically strikes children and young adults. It was then that our family's long struggle with cancer began.

Children with cancer are treated with chemotherapy, radiation, surgery, or some combination of these methods. All cancer treatments are difficult to undergo. But the good news is that survival rates for most forms of childhood cancer continue to improve. More than fifty percent of children with Ewing's sarcoma who are without widespread disease at diagnosis can expect long-term, disease-free survival.

However, cancer challenges not just the patient, but every member of the patient's family. Much of the attention Kathy's brother and sister needed went to Kathy, and sometimes they were resentful. As a working mother and single parent, I was exhausted most of the time, juggling the demands of home, job, and hospital. But for all of us, the biggest challenge was coping with our fear that Kathy would die. One night marked a turning point. We overheard Kathy comforting her brother, saying, "I'm not going to die. You've got to believe that. Believing that will help me more than anything." Like travelers battling a fierce storm, we hung on to the treatment schedule, to each other, and to hope.

Kathy continues to be healthy and active. She swims, dances, reads, draws, and rides her bike. As I watch her grow each day, I am reminded of the special courage that lives in the hearts of all young cancer patients, and I tip my hat to them.

Trudy Krisher